For Emma Tsenti ~ J.W.

To Wendy ~ T.R.

American edition published in 2012 by Andersen Press USA, an imprint of Andersen Press Ltd.
www.andersenpressusa.com

First published in Great Britain in 2012 by Andersen Press Ltd.,
20 Vauxhall Bridge Road, London SW1V 2SA.
Published in Australia by Random House Australia Pty.,
Level 3, 100 Pacific Highway, North Sydney, NSW 2060.
Text copyright © Jeanne Willis, 2012
Illustration copyright © Tony Ross, 2012

Distributed in the United States and Canada by Lerner Publishing Group, Inc.
241 First Avenue North Minneapolis, MN 55401 U.S.A.
www.lernerbooks.com

Color separated in Switzerland by Photolitho AG, Zürich.
Printed and bound in Singapore by Tien Wah Press.
Tony Ross has used pastels in this book.

Library of Congress Cataloging in Publication Data available.
ISBN: 978-1-4677-0314-7

1 – TWP – 3/7/12
This book has been printed on acid-free paper.

Fly, Chick, Fly!

Jeanne Willis   Tony Ross

T 15163

ANDERSEN PRESS USA

In the middle of the wood, there was an oak tree.

In the middle of the oak tree, there was a hole.

In the middle of the hole, there was a nest.

In the middle of the nest, there were three eggs.

In the middle of the eggs, there was an owl . . .

She sat on the eggs all day and night.

For thirty days and nights.

Every dawn, every dusk, Father Owl went
hunting to feed Mother Owl.

When the blossom was in bud, the first chick hatched.

When the blossom was open, the second chick hatched.

When the blossom fell, the third chick hatched.

Ten times a day, Father Owl went hunting.
Ten times a day, Mother Owl fed the chicks.

The chicks grew and grew.

When the blackberries were green,
the first chick tried to fly.
She flapped. She flipped. She flopped . . .
But then she flew!

When the blackberries were ripe,
the second chick tried to fly.
He flapped. He flipped. He flopped . . .
Then he flew too!

The blackberries had gone.

The leaves were turning brown.

But the last chick was still in the nest.

"Fly!" said Mother Owl.

"Not I!" said the last chick.

She would not even try.

"You
must fly!"
said her mother.
"You must fly!"
said her father.

"Why?" said the last chick.

"If I fly, the crow might get me.
If I fly, the rain might wet me.
If I fly, a train might hit me.
My sister flew and never came back.
Why would I want to fly?"

"You belong in the sky," said her mother.
"Your sister is at home in the old elm tree.
Fly, little chick, just try!"

The last chick clung to the end of a branch.
She flapped. She flipped. She flopped . . .

. . . and hopped back into the nest.

"Time to go," said Father Owl.
But the last little chick cried, "No, no, no!
My brother flew and never came back.
Was he eaten by a crow or killed on the track?
Why would I want to fly?"

She flew!

Snow came. Crow came. Spring came.
But what became of this last chick?

In the wood, there is a beech tree.

In the middle of the beech tree, there is a hole.

In the middle of the hole, there is a nest.

In the middle of the nest, there is an owl.

She was the last chick to fly.

But she is glad she flew because . . .

. . . here is *her* first chick!

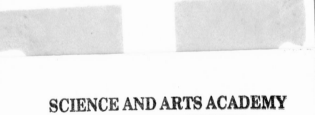

SCIENCE AND ARTS ACADEMY
1825 MINER STREET
DES PLAINES, IL 60016